Dear Lily,
You got this!
Love,
Ms Vykeo Slutzker

This book is dedicated to my three sons,
Michael, Nicholas and Maximillian.
They have taught me the true meaning of unconditional love and have reminded me that ***"I got this."***

Published by

Black Feather PRESS
CONTENT, EDITING & PUBLISHING

All rights reserved. No part of this book may be used without written permission from the publisher.

Nini Bells
She's Got This

Written by
Kris Ufkes-Stertzer

Illustrations by
Maja Martinovic

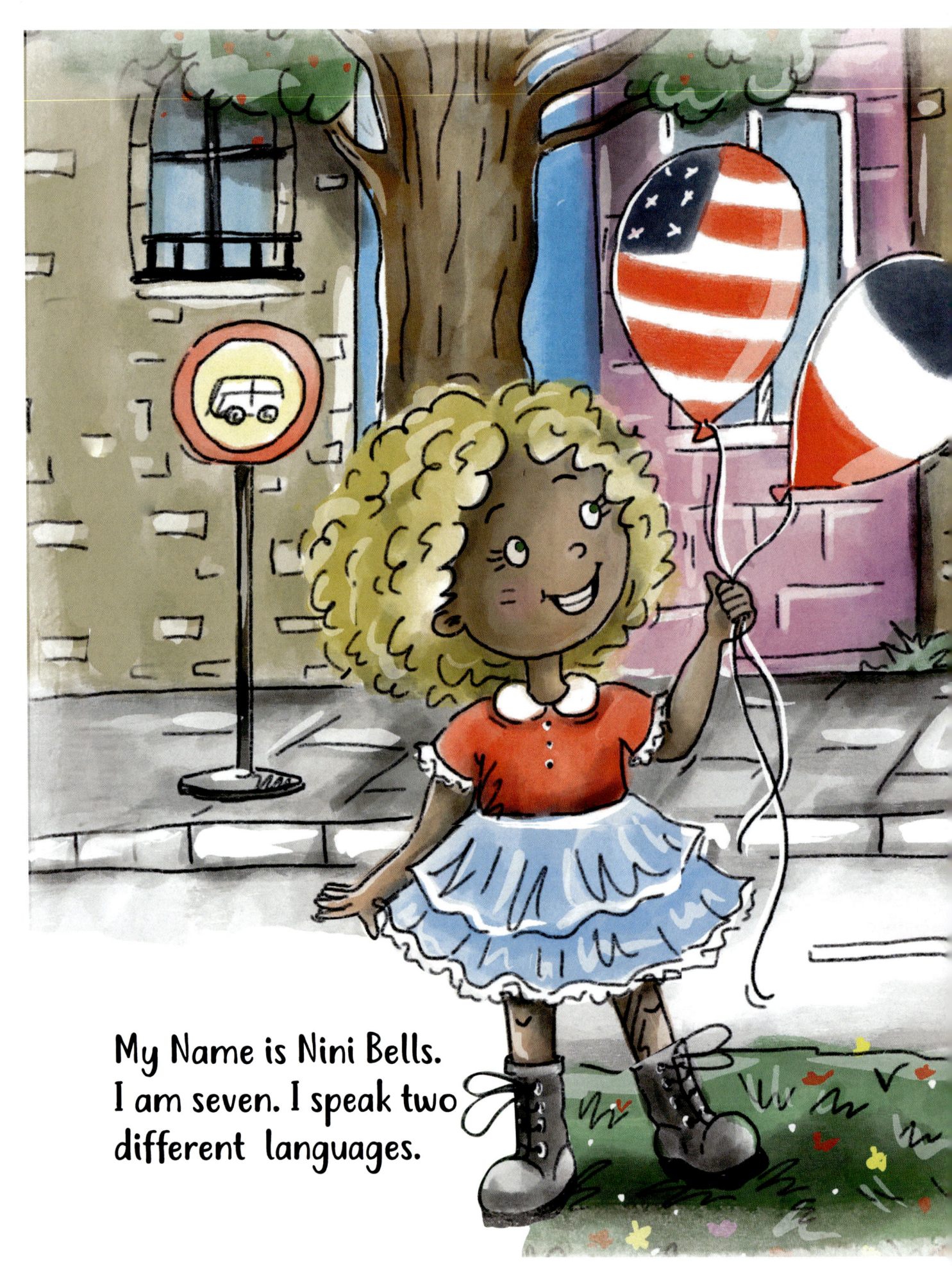

My Name is Nini Bells.
I am seven. I speak two
different languages.

I have big blonde curls and green eyes.
I do not like my curls. I like dresses.
Pants feel itchy. Dresses are my favorite.

I have a nanny.
Her name is Pat.
A nanny is like a mom
or a dad who helps out
with the chores.

My Pat does more than chores.
She jumps rope, rides bikes
and listens to all my secrets.

She lets me sit in her room
while she puts her curlers in at night.
Why would anyone want curls
on purpose?
I do not like them.

I have to leave when it is time for bed.

I say, "Pattycakes, may I sleep here with you?"

Patty says, "no you may not," and directs me to the door.

As she sends me to my room
she says in a pretend stern voice:
"And my name is Pat."

I crawl up the stairs slowly hoping
Patty will change her mind.

Pat says from behind her closed
door, "YOU GOT THIS, Nini!"

"Okay," I sing back in her direction.
But I am not certain.
Singing makes it feel better.

As I crawl into bed I grab Mrs. Lavanski.
She is a blue rubber mouse with
a polka-dotted apron.

My bright yellow room isn't so bright at night.
Mrs. Lavanski sits on the pillow by my side.

Why do all the scary thoughts visit you at night?
Do they know you're alone?

Do they know that my Pat isn't there to protect me?

Why does the night make me worry about tomorrow?

Will I be able to tie my shoe if it should get untied?

Will I be able to walk to school without being afraid?

What If my friend Ruby forgets to pick me up?

Ruby is nine.
She always says, "don't worry. You got this."

What if it rains tomorrow and the wind blows my bubble umbrella so hard and takes me in another direction?

What if my homework gets wet?

What if I'm late for school?

What if my teacher, Mrs. Molisani, asks a question and I can't remember the answer?

What if I don't even understand the question?

I like Mrs. Molisani.
She has beautiful brown hair
and bright blue eyes.
I feel happy around her.

I wish there were a hundred
Patty Cakes and a hundred Mrs. Molisanis.

What if we make rock soup and I have too many sips and then I have to use the little girls' room?

What if I can't make it to the little girls' room?

What if I struggle and can't slip
the button through the hole?

What if I don't have extra pants in my cubby?

What if there are only extra big kid pants to
spare and no little kid pants?

That would be so many, too many "what ifs" for me to worry about in a day!

Mrs. Lavanski says, "You save some of those worries for me, Miss Nini. Worries can be so very heavy at times."

"Thank you, Mrs. Lavanski. That will for sure help!"

My eyes are getting so heavy,
and Mrs. Lavanski is tired too.

Just before I feel the last
"what if" coming from my sleepy voice,
I hear:

"Hey tomorrow, Nini Bells, you got this!"

The next morning the sun is shining in my bright yellow room.

Mrs. Lavanski is still sleeping.

Pat has already been in my room to lay out my favorite soft dress.

I run downstairs and Ruby is already on the front stairs waiting for me.

Pat tells me to scoot and I tell her, "DON'T you worry.

I will be back sooner than you think."

Patty says, "Well, you have a good day, Nini Bells, and remember ..."

"I know, I know," I say, "I got this!"

THE END